READY, SET, GO!

I wish, I wish
With all my heart
To fly with dragons
In a land apart.

By Irene Trimble
Based on a story by Bob Carrau
Illustrated by Don Williams
Based on the characters by Ron Rodecker

Visit Dragon Tales on the Web at www.dragontales.com
Watch us on PBS!

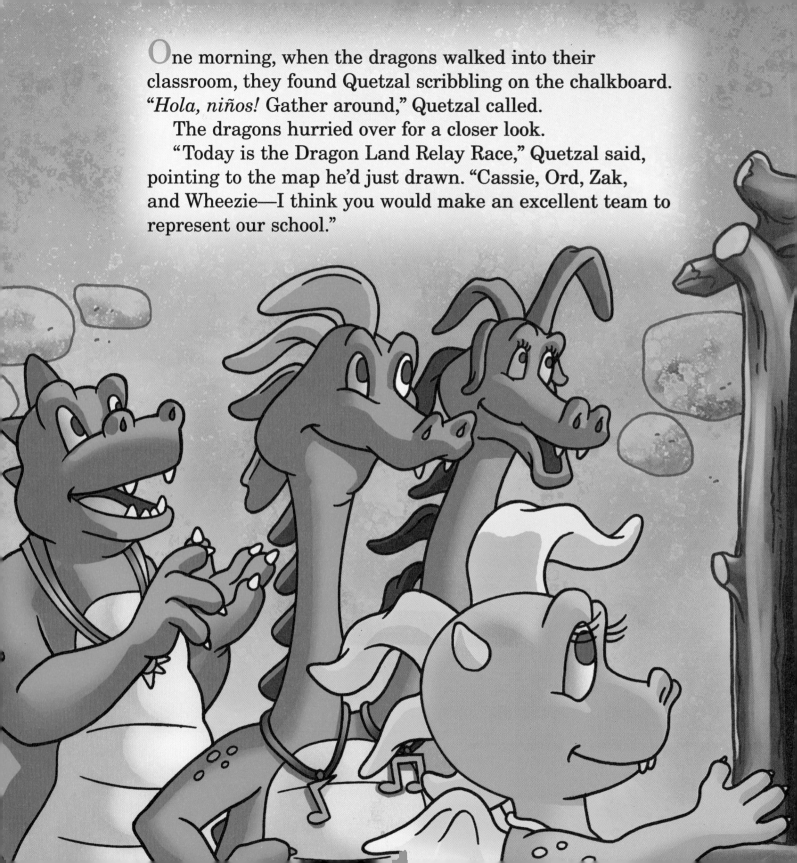

One morning, when the dragons walked into their classroom, they found Quetzal scribbling on the chalkboard. "*Hola, niños!* Gather around," Quetzal called.

The dragons hurried over for a closer look.

"Today is the Dragon Land Relay Race," Quetzal said, pointing to the map he'd just drawn. "Cassie, Ord, Zak, and Wheezie—I think you would make an excellent team to represent our school."

"Of course, you will need someone to lead your team as captain," Quetzal added. "I saw you study the map carefully, Cassie. Will you be the *capitán*?"

"Me?" Cassie answered. She felt proud but nervous. "I'll try to do a good job, Quetzal."

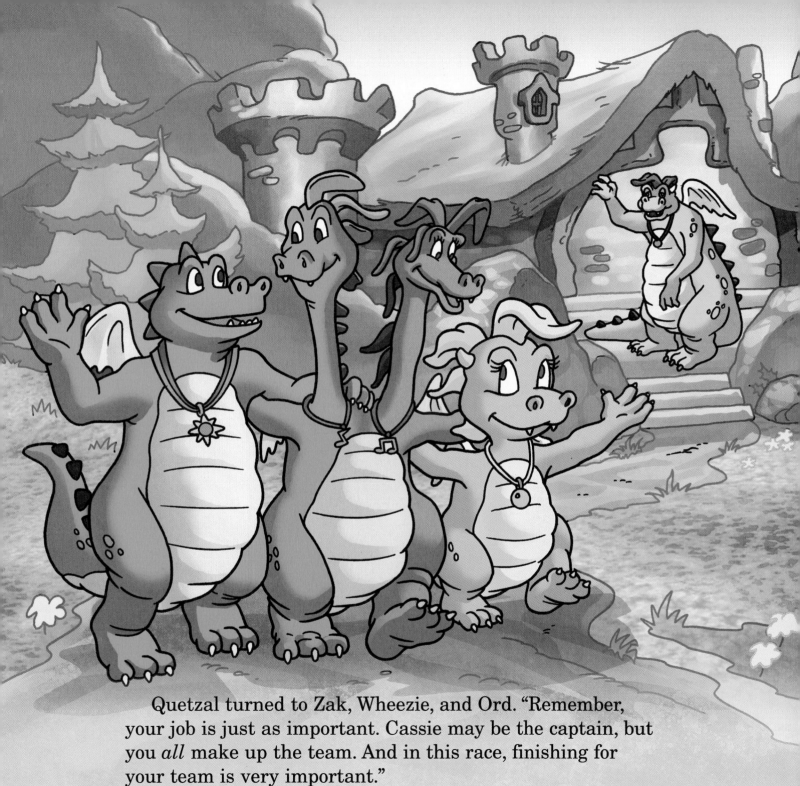

Quetzal turned to Zak, Wheezie, and Ord. "Remember, your job is just as important. Cassie may be the captain, but you *all* make up the team. And in this race, finishing for your team is very important."

So the dragons headed out to the racecourse to practice.

When they reached the racecourse, Ord gulped. "It looks a lot harder than it did on Quetzal's chalkboard!"

"It is a *little* hard, but I know we can do it!" Cassie said. "Zak and Wheezie can start. They'll zigzag through the toadstools."

"Okey-dokey, artichokey!" Wheezie said.

"When they tag my hand, it's my turn," Cassie went on. "I have to jump over the whirling water without getting wet. When I tag Ord, he'll climb the rainbow rock and then race to the finish."

Zak and Wheezie took their places. Cassie shouted, "GO!"
"This way, Wheezie," said Zak, pulling in one direction.
"No, *this* way," snapped Wheezie, pulling the other way.

Captain Cassie stepped in. "Um, guys . . . don't forget we're a team," she reminded them. "You have to decide *together* which way to go."

Zak and Wheezie nodded. "Let's try again," Zak said. "First we'll go your way, Wheezie, then we'll go mine, okay?" This time, the dragons sailed through the toadstools.

Next it was Cassie's turn. She stood in front of the whirling water, watching the geysers bubble into the air.

"Remember, we can't use our wings in relay races," Zak said.

"If I can't use my wings, I don't know if I can do it," Cassie whispered.

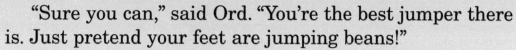

"Sure you can," said Ord. "You're the best jumper there is. Just pretend your feet are jumping beans!"

Cassie giggled. Then she had a great idea. If she had a running start, maybe the jump would be easier. Cassie ran just as fast as she could. "Wheee!" she shouted.

"Thanks!" Cassie told her team. "Now it's your turn, Ord."
Ord stared up at the climbing rock doubtfully. "It looks as tall as Stickleback Mountain," he groaned. Ord grabbed the rope and began to pull himself up the rock. But his hands slipped and—BOOM!—down he tumbled.

One of the dragons from another team giggled as Ord bounced on the soft mushrooms piled at the foot of the rock.

"Ouch!" cried Ord. "That hurt!"

But it was plain to see that his feelings were what hurt the most.

"I'm *not* climbing that dumb rock again!" Ord shouted. He stormed off, sniffling, while Cassie followed.

"I can't climb the rock," said Ord. "I can't help the team."

"You helped me jump over the water," said Cassie.
"Maybe the team can help you climb the rock."
"You can?" He sounded hopeful. "How?"
Cassie smiled. "Come on and see!"

So Ord stood at the bottom of the climbing rock once again.
This time, Cassie coached him. "Bounce on the mushrooms
to give yourself a boost."

"It's easier if you use your legs to climb, too," Zak told him.

"Try your toes!" added Wheezie. "Mine are super-grabby!"

Sure enough, to his amazement, Ord was climbing higher. But he was still nowhere near the top when Quetzal shouted that the real race was about to begin. Ord jumped to the ground. "Don't worry, I can finish," he told the team. "I *think*. . . ."

The dragons took their places on the course. The teams all wished each other luck. Then came the trumpet flower's noisy "Tootle-oo-hoot." The race had begun!

Zak and Wheezie dashed to the toadstools. They wobbled for a moment, first right, then left. But then they glided through, and Zak tagged Cassie's hand. Sprays of water tried to tickle her toes, but Cassie sailed over the waterspouts.

When Cassie tagged Ord, he took a deep breath. Slowly, he started to climb. The other racers passed him as if they were flying.

"Don't give up," Ord whispered to himself. "I can't fly, but I *can* try!"

The other racers reached the top of the rock and ran for the finish line. Ord didn't even watch.

"Almost . . . there," he puffed.

Cassie, Quetzal, and Zak and Wheezie cheered wildly as Ord hauled himself to the very tiptop.

"I did it! I did it!" Ord shouted, jumping up and down.
Ord had forgotten about the rest of the race!
"Good job, Ord!" Cassie shouted. "Now race to the finish."
Ord charged toward the finish line with the whole crowd
cheering him on.

As Ord crossed the finish line, his team gave him a big hug.
"I'm sorry we came in last," Ord panted.
"Isn't it funny?" Wheezie said. "It feels like we won!"
Cassie smiled at her team. "We did! We all worked together to finish. When a team does that, you know what they are?"
"Winners!" shouted Ord. "Every time!"